Doub

The ball was on the floor beside me. I grabbed it.

"Let's see how you like it, muscle-head!" I yelled, and threw the ball as hard as I could toward D.K.

It hit Mr. Rambeau instead.

I couldn't believe it. I ran out of that gym as fast as I could, and all the way home.

I let myself into our apartment and flopped down on the couch. My heart pounded so hard and loud, it echoed through all the rooms.

It took a long time to quiet down. What was I going to do? I'd never get out of this one. Things couldn't get any worse.

I needed to go to the bathroom. The door was closed. I opened it and walked in. I was almost beside the toilet when I saw it.

Three feet of snake was hanging out of the toilet bowl, over the seat, and onto the floor. And it was coming right toward me.

THERE'S A SNAKE IN THE TOILET

Gisela Tobien Sherman

A MINSTREL® BOOK

Published by POCKET BOOKS

New York   London   Toronto   Sydney   Singapore

A MINSTREL PAPERBACK *Original*

A Minstrel Book published by
POCKET BOOKS, a division of Simon & Schuster Inc.
1230 Avenue of the Americas, New York, NY 10020

ISBN: 0-671-87089-0

First Minstrel Books printing June 1995

10 9 8 7 6 5

A MINSTREL BOOK and colophon are registered trademarks of Simon & Schuster Inc.

Cover art by Jeff Mangiat

Printed in the U.S.A.

This book is dedicated to my mother,
Anneliese Wessberge Tobien,
with love and thanks and admiration.

The author wishes to thank Rick and Dan
at The Ark Pet Shop in Hamilton,
and the staff at the Hamilton SPCA,
for their information and advice.

Chapter

1

"THERE'S A HURRICANE WARNING ON. I CAN'T GO out for recess this afternoon."

"No, Ollie. It's a sunny, clear day. Out you go."

"I have a terrible cough, Mrs. McPinkle. Uwuuh, uwuuh."

"The fresh air will be good for it." Mrs. McPinkle took a long, deep breath, pushed her glasses up on her nose, and smiled at me hopefully.

"My math problems! I've got to finish them." I can't believe I said that.

"They'll wait for you. Now get out there, or I'll give you double recess."

Mrs. McPinkle patted my back and steered me out the classroom door. I shuffled down the hall as slowly as I could. Then, as she turned to walk in the opposite direction toward the teachers' room, I ducked into the boys' washroom. It doesn't always smell so great, but recess in there is better than outside on that playground.

I bumped into a pair of hairy thick legs and brown shorts. Just my luck—Mr. Rambeau, the gym teacher, was still on duty.

"Sullivan!" he bellowed at me like an army sergeant. "You're late. Get moving."

Through the frosted washroom windows, I could see the shapes of kids running around the playground. I could hear them screeching, teasing, screaming. Today it would be worse.

Somewhere out there was D.K. His expression would be so innocent, but his left hand would stay in his pocket, hiding *it*, until someone got close enough. I could not go out there.

Mr. Rambeau pulled impatiently at his thick mustache, and stood waiting. He would never understand. He was too big and muscled and tough. I had to think fast.

"Mrs. McPinkle sent me in here to make sure that everyone has cleared out. I have to report back to her right away." I hate the way my voice gets squeaky when I talk to him.

I raced back out of the swinging door, into the hall, and smack into a scratchy blue dress. Mrs. McPinkle. I was stuck.

"And where do you think you're going, young man?"

"Um . . . ah . . ."

I turned desperately from an angry face with big round glasses to an angry face with a shaggy mustache.

"Every child in school loves recess, Ollie. Why don't you?"

I turned back to Mrs. McPinkle. She stared at me, waiting for an answer. She stepped closer. Her eyes looked ten times bigger behind her glasses. I felt like a tiny bug shivering under a microscope. Should I just dodge around them and take off? I could race out of the school and never come back.

3

I glanced back the other way. Mr. Rambeau's hairy legs looked at least five feet long. I'd never make it. If only I were in Egypt with my dad.

"Sullivan, we're waiting for an answer," he roared.

"It's a war zone out there. Everyone thinks they're a ninja or a Power Ranger. They jump, push, kick, and hit—even the girls," I answered.

Mr. Rambeau's mouth curled up so it looked like his mustache was growing out of his nose. He grunted with disgust and stomped off down the hall.

Mrs. McPinkle started her speech about how running away never solved problems. I was thinking that it sure solved mine. Just then the recess bell rang. Recess was over. I was saved.

The noise of kids rushing in stopped her speech. She waved me away and reached to grab two big guys still punching each other.

I watched D.K. walk in. He would have looked tough even without his spiked hair and the earring hanging from his dirty ear.

4

He had the biggest fists and the fastest temper in grade five. Nobody messed with D.K.

D.K.'s hand wiggled in his pocket and no one went near him. He was grinning wider than a toothpaste commercial. When he saw me, he waved with his free hand.

"Hey, Ollie. I missed you at recess. C'mere."

I started to walk away, trying to look cool.

Why didn't any teachers, who see everything else, see what D.K. had? Why couldn't they just turn around, in time to catch him with the snake out of his pocket?

Lots of other kids were scared too. Why wouldn't anyone tell on him? Because no one wanted to be a tattletale.

D.K. came closer. He pulled his hand out of his pocket. Yech. I could see it, slithering between his fingers. It was slimy and green and mean looking. Its slitty yellow eyes gleamed hungrily at me.

My mouth went dry. My heart felt like a heavy-metal drummer was banging on it. It's not my fault I'm terrified of snakes. It runs in my family.

I panicked and bolted into my classroom. Ouch! I bashed my leg against the edge of a desk.

D.K.'s laughter echoed down the hall. I'd escaped—this time. But he knew, and I knew, that sooner or later today I would have to come face to fang with that snake.

But I was more worried about something else.

It's bad enough to be scared of a snake, but I knew that D.K. would tease me with it until I cried—in front of all the other kids. They'd love it.

It would be another good chance to chase me around, laughing and singing, "Bawlie Ollie. Wah-wah. Baw-lie Ol-lie Sull-i-van."

Chapter

2

RUNNING AWAY FROM PROBLEMS MAY NOT MAKE you brave, but it sure forces you to be smart. I managed to keep away from D.K. and his snake for the rest of the day in school.

My biggest worry now was how was I going to get home safely? Things were tough enough before D.K. moved into our building to live with his grandmother. Now they're downright dangerous.

My usual trick—staying after school until the bullies are gone—wouldn't work today. The teachers were having a meeting and sent us all out at the same time. I almost wished my mother were there to pick me up.

No. That's what started my troubles in the first place. She worries too much about me. She used to walk me to school—and pick me up—every day. She said she didn't care that I was ten years old.

"Oh, Oliver, you'll still be my baby when you're ninety-three," she always says.

The day she started work and stopped taking me to school and back, I was the happiest kid in grade five.

Even though he doesn't live with us anymore, my dad helped my sister and me get some more freedom. He had yelled at my mother over the phone, so loud that we heard him. "Inge. A ten-year-old boy and his twelve-year-old sister can stay home alone after school for thirty minutes until you get there."

I knew I'd have to depend on fast footwork and my secret routes to get home. I know every alley and store and hiding place for a square mile around.

I had just sneaked in the front and out the back door of Dandy's Candies. There was one last block to go. Then I would be home free.

8

This was the toughest block though, because it was a large, empty lot. There was no place to hide.

I looked left. I searched right. I took a deep breath. And another. Then I scorched across that lot as if ten rattlesnakes were behind me.

There was my building. I was safe.

No, I wasn't.

In the front parking lot stood a circle of kids. Everyone in the circle was staring at D.K. He grinned wickedly. Why was he so happy?

He was swinging his skinny green snake in front of him, back and forth, slowly. All the time he was moving closer and closer toward little Laura-Lee Cheng.

Laura-Lee looked terrified. Her lips were shut in a tight white line. The brick apartment wall blocked her from moving farther back. The kids were all around her. She was cornered.

I stopped and watched, frozen with fascination, just like the other kids.

Now D.K. acted as if the snake were a

9

sword. He jumped around and jabbed it toward her. Its tail curled up to his thumb. How could he stand holding that thing?

Poor Laura-Lee. She looked around for help. Not one of us could offer it. We were afraid to be next.

D.K. threw the snake. It hit Laura-Lee in the face, then dropped to her shoulder. It lay there in rows of frilly white lace. Its mouth pointed at her neck.

I thought I would be sick.

Little Laura-Lee lifted her chin. Her horrified face became calm. She seemed to grow taller. She stood as still as a queen, and looked at D.K. as if he were toe jam.

Slowly, with great cool, she reached toward her shoulder. She pulled off the snake and dropped it daintily into the middle of some bushes. It slithered quickly out of sight. With her head held high, she walked past the others and into the building.

I wished I had courage like that. I wanted to clap, but I was too afraid of D.K. He had been made a fool of by a seven-year-old girl. Now he'd be dangerous. Before anyone noticed me, I raced around the side of the building and in through another door.

I ran down the hall and around the corner. Wow.

I almost crashed into the weirdest thing. The humongous rear end of a pair of acid-dyed jeans was sticking up in the air from the floor. It belonged to Borko, a guy who lives above us, on the second floor. What was he doing down here, on his hands and knees, peering into an air vent?

As soon as he saw me, he jumped up. He narrowed his green eyes into nasty slits, and hissed at me, "Scram, ya little wimp."

I don't think he likes me. I didn't care. I had escaped D.K. The snake had escaped D.K. and disappeared. He could never bother me with it again. My worries were over.

After supper that night I took the garbage to the garbage room down the hall. I pulled open the door, and there was Borko again. This time his head was almost in the chute. He quickly stuffed a flashlight into his pocket.

11

Borko is not the kind of guy you want to meet in a dim little garbage room. Actually, you wouldn't want to meet him anywhere.

He's pretty tough. A thick red scar rips across his cheek. One and a half of his two front teeth are missing. That could be why he hisses when he talks.

He wore a black sweatshirt with the sleeves cut off, so you could see his tattoo. It was of a giant blue snake, coiled around the muscled top of his arm. Its tail pointed down and its head twisted upward. The jaws opened wide to show fangs the size of daggers.

"H-hi, Borko," I squeaked. "What's goin' down?"

He hissed at me and pushed past me down the hall.

When I got back to our apartment, my mom was reading the newspaper out loud to my sister. I knew it. It was another article about a weird accident—some kids had been hurt on a playground.

Kathleen pretended that she was concentrating on her homework. She rolled her eyes up at me till the whites showed. We both knew the list of warnings was coming next.

I ran by my mom with a flying kiss at her cheek, yelled "Good night," and sped into my room.

What a tough day. I was glad to crawl into bed and fall asleep quickly.

It was three o'clock. I woke up and my room was as dark as a cave. The O's on my digital clock glared at me like two beady red eyes. At three-oh-one I got up to go to the washroom.

I was still half-asleep, so I waited until I got into the bathroom before I turned on the hall light. That way I could see without a sudden bright light blinding me.

I lifted the toilet lid. I picked up the seat. Two beady yellow eyes glared at me. I blinked and looked again.

Something dark was curled up in the toilet bowl. The two eyes stared up at me still. They did not blink.

A snake?

A snake!

There was a snake in the toilet! It was not like D.K.'s little green one. This one was enormous. My screams must have woken up the block.

Footsteps pounded down the hall. My mother and Kathleen rushed in and the light flashed on.

I was still frozen to the spot in front of the toilet, screeching. My mom grabbed me and checked for blood.

"What's wrong? Oliver, honey. What happened?" She was almost hysterical, too.

Kathleen has seen too many movies. She slapped me across the face. I stopped yelling just as she was winding up for another blow.

"A snake!" I screamed at them. "There's a snake in the toilet!"

We all looked down at the toilet bowl. There was nothing there except murky water. I jumped back and checked the floor. Nothing.

Kathleen looked disgusted and headed back to her bed. My mom didn't seem too thrilled, either.

She led me back to my bed like I was a baby moron. She sat with me and rubbed my back, telling me I had had a nightmare. By the time she left my room, I sort of believed her.

Then I remembered. I still had to go to the bathroom. Badly. There was no way I'd go now.

It took me a long time to get to sleep again. Had I seen a snake in our toilet? Nah. It was dark. I'd been half-asleep. I have a wild imagination.

It couldn't have been. Whoever heard of a snake in the toilet?

Chapter

3

THE NEXT DAY, THURSDAY, STARTED OUT SO well. How did it end up being the worst day of my life?

I woke up extra early because I was desperate to go to the bathroom. Then I remembered why. The snake. I really hoped that it had been a nightmare.

I tiptoed across the hall. Carefully, I peered into the bathroom. Nothing.

Dum-dum, I told myself. What did you expect—a cobra brushing his fangs? A hippo in the bathtub? I forced myself to march right in. Straight to the toilet.

"See, I am brave," I said out loud, just to break the silence.

At that point I was glad to be a boy. My job could be done standing up, with my eyes on the toilet bowl. There would be no surprises coming up behind me.

It was still early, so I played some computer games for a while. It was fun to be a hero for a change. Then I ate my favorite cereal and poured extra sugar all over it.

I felt so good, I put on my special T-shirt with the picture of a pyramid on it. My dad brought it all the way from Egypt, the last time I saw him. Now he's back there working on a dam again and I won't see him for months.

We had such a great time that last day he visited us. We explored the zoo, where he pointed out all the animals that live in Egypt.

He talked about his dam on the Nile River, and called it "the chance of a lifetime."

I lied about all my friends at school and all the sports I'm great at. He looked at me sort of funny, but didn't say anything. Then he ruffled my hair and sighed.

I was still cheerful when I walked to school that morning. It was the kind of sunny May morning that made you hopeful. School was over in five weeks. Maybe my dad would change his mind and let me spend the summer with him in Egypt.

I didn't expect trouble from D.K. today. Maybe I'd even go out for recess.

Everything stayed fine until lunchtime. Nobody had really teased me. D.K. was quiet and grumpy and minded his own business. I should have remembered he was like a volcano. I should have remembered how fast his fists and his temper exploded the day somebody asked him why he lived with his grandmother.

After lunch we were sent outside. I stood leaning peacefully against the climbing bars, watching the kids on the tires horse around.

"Watch out!"

Ian MacDougall slipped off the tires and crashed toward me. I jumped back.

"Aaugh! You jerk! Look what you did."

It was D.K. I had bumped into him.

"My dessert! You creep. You've wrecked my dessert."

I peered into D.K.'s furious face, then stared at a lumpy mess of cherry pie on the gravel. Boy, was I in trouble.

My luck still held. There was a teacher on duty nearby. She walked over to us, so D.K. had to play it cool. He stomped over to the side of the playground and sulked.

The volcano was getting ready to explode.

There were only two minutes to go before the bell rang. I was a nervous wreck. Was I going to make it? I scanned the playground. It was crowded with every kid in the school. I couldn't see any teachers. I didn't see D.K.

He jumped out and blocked me. I gasped so hard I almost choked. Some other guys noticed the action, and gathered around to watch us.

"Ollie, old buddy, you missed something interesting yesterday. I was saving it for you, but unfortunately I lost it. Luckily, I found something else."

19

I was petrified. How had he found another snake so fast?

Closer and closer he stepped. He stuck out his hand. I was so relieved, I almost laughed out loud. He held a caterpillar. A little brown caterpillar. It was curled up in a fuzzy frightened ball.

More guys saw D.K. and me, and the circle around us. They figured there was a fight going on, and ran over to see it. A crowd grew around us—waiting.

I was all right. D.K.'s little caterpillar didn't scare me. This was my chance to prove myself. I made a big show of shrugging my shoulders. In my toughest voice I yelled, "Gee thanks, D.K. I love caterpillars. I've got some at home, even bigger."

Then, seeing all those kids watching, I added, "Watch out it doesn't do number two on your hand."

Our audience laughed. They liked me! It felt great.

D.K. heard the laughter too. His face scrunched up mad, and he charged me. In a flash, he had dropped the caterpillar down the inside of my T-shirt.

"You like him, he's yours!" he shouted.

It tickled as it crawled across my chest. I didn't like it, but I kept up my show.

"Thanks. I'll keep it for a pet. I'll call it Dilmar."

I'd gone too far. The few kids who know D.K.'s real name, also know how much he hates it. Who can blame him?

He charged me like a crazy rhinoceros. He pounded my chest with both fists. I fell backward and landed on the ground. D.K. stayed on top of me, still punching.

By the time a teacher pulled him off, it was too late. He had squashed the caterpillar on my chest. A large mess of green and yellow splattered and stained the front of my T-shirt. My special T-shirt from my dad, whom I wouldn't see again for a whole year.

I lay in the dirt and my dad's smile flashed in front of me. He had said, "Think of me when you wear that, son."

Before I knew it, tears had filled my eyes and rolled down my cheeks. I had forgotten

21

about the kids around us. Then I heard the giggles.

By the time I could make the tears stop, everybody was laughing. I got up and wiped the dust and gravel off myself. My big moment had come—and I'd blown it.

My nose was bleeding. The teacher on duty handed me a tissue to wipe the dirt and tears and blood off my face.

"Go inside and clean yourself up."

She looked sorry for me. Then she tried to quiet the kids, but they got even louder.

"Bawlie Ollie. Bawlie Ollie. BAWLIE OLLIE."

It sounded like the whole world was chanting it as I ran into the school.

I could hear them through the closed bathroom window, while I cleaned the stuff off my T-shirt and chest.

I was doomed for life. Before, when the guys called me Bawlie Ollie, there hadn't really been a reason. It just sounded good. (Maybe I did cry once in kindergarten.) Now I was Bawlie Ollie to everyone—forever.

"Why wasn't I called Matt or Hulk?" I yelled at the mirror.

"You think you've got it bad? Try going through life called Gawa Luciano Cheng."

In the mirror, I saw the reflection of Laura-Lee's big brother. His black hair stuck straight out in the wrong places. He wore the biggest, shiniest braces in the world, but his eyes were always smiling. He washed his hands beside me. With a wave and a smile, he headed out the bathroom door.

The bell rang. If I went in last to class, I'd be the center of attention some more. I forced myself to join the crowd in the hall.

It was a terrible afternoon. I heard "Bawlie Ollie" whispered everywhere. Someone tripped me when I walked up the aisle to go to the blackboard.

"Why was Ollie crying?" asked Zoe, who is the prettiest, most decent girl in our class.

" 'Cause he's afraid of caterpillars," someone told her.

She looked at me like I was a nerd from outer space.

I had had enough, but then I had to go to gym with Mr. Rambeau.

By the way he glanced at me, I could tell he'd heard what had happened. I could also tell what he thought of me.

"Sullivan! Boys lift their knees off the floor for push-ups. Do twenty more."

"Sullivan, catch the ball like a boy. Don't duck."

We played dodgeball. When Rambeau wasn't looking, D.K. slammed the ball at me, right where it really hurts.

I scrunched over in pain. My eyes stung. If I held myself together tightly enough, I could keep myself from crying.

"What's wrong with Sullivan?" Mr. Rambeau finally noticed.

"I don't know, sir. I think the ball hit his knee," answered D.K. and he glared at the others, daring them to tell the truth.

Rambeau's mustache went up to his nose again.

"For pete's sake, boy. Toughen up. And don't turn on the waterworks again."

The pain was like a hammer in my shorts.

Once again there was a circle of kids around me, laughing. It was all so unfair. I was afraid I'd burst into tears. I had to do something.

I got mad.

The ball was on the floor beside me. I grabbed it.

"Let's see how you like it, muscle-head!" I yelled, and threw the ball toward D.K. as hard as I could.

It hit Mr. Rambeau exactly where it had hit me.

The other guys looked like baby robins in shock, their eyes and mouths open wide. They weren't as surprised as I was.

I couldn't even look at Mr. Rambeau. I ran out of that gym. Out of the school. All the way home.

I let myself into our apartment and flopped down on the couch. My heart pounded so hard and loud, it echoed through all the rooms.

It took a long time to quiet down. Every time I thought about what I had done, my heart started pounding again.

Finally I was calm. The telephone rang like

a police siren. The school. They were calling home already. Next they'd try my mother at work.

What was I going to do? I'd never get out of this one. Things couldn't get any worse.

I needed to go to the bathroom. The door was closed. I opened it and walked in. I was almost beside the toilet when I noticed it.

Three feet of snake was hanging out of the toilet bowl, over the seat, and onto the floor. It was coming toward me.

Chapter

4

I TURNED AND RAN, WAILING LIKE A FIRE ENGINE.
Well, what would you have done?

Before I knew it, I was halfway down the
hall, still screeching. Mrs. Capelli grabbed
me.

"A snake!" I yelled at her. "A snake's chasing me!"

"A snake? Where?"

"The toilet. He's coming out of the toilet."

She looked mad enough to hit me. "You
kids and your stupid jokes. One day you'll
give someone a heart attack." She stomped
back to her apartment and slammed the
door.

By then, some other people were opening their doors, asking what was going on. Mrs. Krokowski decided to believe me. She got as far as our bathroom door.

Only the top foot of the snake was sticking out of the toilet now. Its eyes glittered greeny yellow. Its tongue flicked out and in.

Mrs. Krokowski groaned and fainted. She hit the floor hard. Her face was so white, I screamed out into the hall again.

"That's it, you little hoodlum. You're supposed to be in school, not terrorizing the neighbors. I'm calling the police." Mrs. Capelli was furious.

"No! Get help. Mrs. Krokowski's fainted in our bathroom."

She had already slammed her door, but a few other people had come out into the hall. Everyone was asking questions.

Some followed me in to Mrs. Krokowski. Only Professor Singh, who was right behind me, saw the last of the snake disappear in a splash of water. Everyone else was running around in three directions—looking for water, for fresh air, for smelling salts. Who keeps smelling salts in a house nowadays?

A while later Miss Longboat, who used to be a nurse, was helping Mrs. Krokowski sit up. She was still deathly white. A bump the size of an apple had risen on the side of her head.

"Get me out of here," she wailed. "I'm not staying in this room with that horrible snake!"

Everyone looked around the bathroom nervously. "Let's get this woman out to the living room for more air," someone said.

All of them ran for the bathroom door so fast, they got jammed in the doorway. It was a mess of arms and legs and elbows. Then someone remembered to go back for Mrs. Krokowski.

"Now, what's going on in here, eh?"

Zoom Zoubek, the superintendent, shuffled over to us.

Seven people told him—all at the same time. They were drowned out by the wail of sirens. Closer and louder they came until they stopped outside our building.

29

Zoom Zoubek ran to the window. "The police! Now I run a clean building here, eh. What have you done, eh?"

Seven people told him again—all at the same time again. Two police officers, the size of blue spruce trees, filled our open door.

"Is this where the boy is holding a wild party?" one of them demanded.

I could see Mrs. Capelli, peering out from behind them.

They came inside, carefully. Eight people circled them, telling them what had happened.

They were drowned out by another siren. Everyone rushed to the window this time.

"An ambulance! And there's another police car with it."

Soon two men rushed in with a stretcher.

"Someone's collapsed in here?" asked the bald one.

By now the hall was full of people. Their heads were bobbing left and right, trying to see. Questions flew through the hall like mosquitoes at a barbecue.

The people with the most nerve tramped right into our apartment. Everybody talked at once. Someone knocked over a plant. Broken bits of clay and earth scattered over the rug. Someone else stepped on it.

Our new beige rug. My mother would have a fit. My mother!

She'd be coming home from work any minute now! My mother, who holds her breath until we get back from the corner store. My mother, who makes us wear boots till May, and still pins our address inside our pockets. My mother was about to come home to see two police cars, an ambulance, and a horde of people in front of her apartment.

"Get out! Everything's all right! The snake's gone. Go home," I yelled at everyone. I even pushed a few toward the door.

No one budged. They were all too busy talking.

Then I heard the scream down the hall, at the front lobby.

"My babies! Oliver! Kathleen! What's happened?"

Her hair and coat were flying. Her eyes were huge and glassy.

My mother had come home.

Chapter

5

My mom is funny. She fusses and panics when there's nothing wrong, but, boy, is she cool during an emergency.

By the time Kathleen came home, Mom had cleared out the apartment, given the police officers a statement, and called the S.P.C.A. She made me clean up the plant mess.

"I got a long, nasty call from school today, Oliver. We'll discuss that later."

Oh no. I'd almost forgotten about that.

We were explaining everything to Kathleen, when the buzzer sounded.

It was a man from the S.P.C.A. Officer Pat

Piper had curly brown hair, a long nose, and droopy brown eyes. He was like a hound dog who'd been left at the pound too long. He also looked like he didn't believe me about the snake. He followed us to the bathroom anyway.

He peeked and poked around the toilet. I half-expected him to start sniffing at it. Then he sat on the edge of the bathtub and stared at me, eye-level.

"Now, sonny, tell me what happened. Exactly what did you see?" he said.

I tried to tell him, but he kept interrupting me with questions. I wanted to offer to take a lie detector test, but my mom was listening.

Mrs. Krokowski and Professor Singh came over to tell him what they had seen.

"It was a boa constrictor, I'm sure," said Professor Singh. "I saw the last bit of it. I could tell by the pale brown color and his markings, like chocolate brown triangles. He's not yet full-grown."

"How big is full-grown?" I asked.

"Only about six or eight feet," said Officer Piper. "They're the smallest of the big snakes."

33

"Only!" Kathleen gulped for air. "That's six or eight feet more snake than I want in my bathroom."

She turned to my mother and wailed, "I can't use this bathroom. What if that snake creeps up and gets me? What am I going to do?"

"We'll use the Krokowskis' bathroom, across the hall. I'm sure they'll let us. Now, Officer Piper, how are you going to get that thing out of our toilet?"

Officer Piper scratched his head. "He's been frightened away by all the noise. He could be in the main sewer system by now. He might be in someone else's toilet, or even behind their wallboards."

"But what if it's still here?"

"Let's try pouring warm water in the toilet. The warmer water should attract the boa back up here. Then I'll grab him."

We poured in enough warm water to float a crocodile. We waited. It was like watching a really bad horror movie. I was afraid to look at the toilet, yet I couldn't help sneaking peeks at it.

Kathleen went to her room. "I'm not having anything to do with this. It's too disgusting. Why would I want to see a stupid snake, anyway?"

She walked past the bathroom forty-seven times in the next hour.

At six-thirty Officer Piper packed up his papers and said, "Good-bye. I'll call in the morning to see how you are managing."

"Good-bye? Why are you leaving?" My mom was shocked.

"There's nothing else I can do here right now. My shift is over. I'm going home for supper."

"Supper!" My mom was mad. "What do you mean, supper? We have a killer snake in our bathroom and you want to go home for supper?"

They argued for a while. My mom won the argument, but he still went home for supper.

We stood and looked at one another—my mom, Kathleen, and me. We realized there wasn't anything we could do—except get our supper. Kathleen shut the bathroom door and we walked to the kitchen.

Before we even got a can of soup open, the first of the visitors was at the door.

"Inge? Did they get it?" Mom's friend from the third floor stepped in as if there were snakes lurking behind every piece of furniture. They talked at fast-forward speed.

"Warm water? Forget it. Why would you want him to come up now? He'll crush you all while you're asleep."

Aughhhh. I hadn't thought of that.

"Boiling water. Pour in hot boiling water. That'll keep it away."

The Singhs came in next. "Close the toilet seat lid. Put a heavy box on top of it. He can't get out that way."

Mr. Stoker told us, "Put some food in the toilet. When he comes up for it, grab him."

It was amazing how many people that night knew exactly how to catch a boa. All we had to do was grab him. Ha-ha.

D.K.'s grandmother insisted, "Drain Blaster. You pour a full can of Drain Blaster down there. It'll eat'm up in minutes. Won't be botherin' you no more."

I could see where D.K. got his kind heart.

"I've already poured some in mine, just in case," she said. She took a crumpled-looking cigarette out of her housecoat pocket and lit it. A huge gray cloud of smoke blew across the hall at us. "And I'm charging the landlord for it. He's got his nerve, lettin' a deadly snake endanger our lives like this."

There was one good thing about all these smart visitors. My mom couldn't talk to me about the phone call from school.

Finally, by nine-thirty, they were all gone. We took turns going over to use the Krokowskis' bathroom. I felt really dumb walking past all the Krokowskis watching TV in their living room, holding my towel and toothpaste and Snoopy toothbrush.

Mom was waiting for me when I got back to my room.

"I still can't believe what I heard from your principal today."

"She probably exaggerated. They always make it sound worse than it really is."

"What can be worse than swearing at a teacher and attacking him?"

"See, I told you. That's blown way—"

37

"Oliver! This is serious—"

"But let me explain. I didn't mean—"

"I'm sure you had some reason, but there is no reason good enough to attack a teacher."

"Attack! I threw a little ball at him. The same one he makes us throw at each other."

"Don't argue with me. You're in enough trouble already."

"How much trouble?"

My mom stopped cold. Her nose twitched and her eyes got all red and wet. "You're suspended from school. My own son kicked out of school."

"Suspended? Forever?" (Me? I couldn't believe it.)

"Three days. Then we have to go talk to the principal and the teacher you hit."

"I didn't hit him."

"Well, exactly what did you do? Explain it to me, Ollie."

I thought back to my horrible day. How far back should I explain? How could I make her know what it felt like to see green caterpillar guts all over Dad's T-shirt—to cry in front of the whole school that thinks you're

38

a wimp anyway, Mr. Rambeau never letting up on me, the pain of that dodge ball? I was still trying to think of where to start and what to say when my mom started to cry.

"You can't tell me. You wish you had your dad to talk to. Well, I wish you did, too. But he's left us. He's not here, and I am, and I'm doing my best. . . ."

I hugged her. We sat together on the edge of my bed for a long time.

Next morning the phone rang early and woke me up from an awful nightmare. I had been running, running. A gigantic snake with toilet paper wound around him like a winter scarf was chasing me. I was trying to get away, but my feet were too heavy to move. Then D.K. chased both of us, yelling, "Pour Drain Blaster on them."

By the time I got to the kitchen, my mom had already answered the second telephone call. The neighbors were checking to see if we'd caught the snake yet.

Did they think we had Tarzan helping us?

My mom pulled the telephone jack out of the

wall. Five minutes later someone knocked at the door.

Officer Pat Piper was the fifth guy at the door. He carried a small yellow poster and looked mad.

"Who put this sign up in the hall?"

I read it quickly. It was a warning about a deadly snake loose in the building. I didn't know who had put it up.

"We're trying to keep this as quiet as possible. We want to avoid a major panic."

There was another knock at the door. Quiet? Who was he kidding?

My mom had to leave for work and Kathleen went to school.

I was left home with a bunch of chores, a ton of schoolwork my mom had made up, a snake in my toilet—and a frozen rat.

I'm not joking. Officer Piper held a white rat, frozen and packed in a little plastic bag. A red $1.99 sticker was stuck on it.

"You can buy them at Noah's Pet Shop," he explained. "People feed them to their pet snakes."

He unwrapped the rat, rolled up his sleeves,

and sat down beside the toilet. Holding the rat, he stuck his left hand in the water.

"The rat is bait. The smell should make the boa hungry. It'll come up, bite the rat, and I'll pull him out. Snake's caught. Problem solved. Case closed."

It sounded too easy to me.

I hung around to watch. Then I started thinking. I imagined Officer Piper pulling the snake out of the john. A snake that long would take a lot of force. Once it came loose, it would come flying out of there and whip around like a lasso. I did not want to be in the path of that lasso.

What if he needed my help in pulling it out? What if the snake bit his hand instead of the rat? Then I'd have to help him. Could I pull the snake's fangs out of Officer Piper's flesh? Touch that snake? Watch the blood spurt? Yech, no. I left the bathroom to clean up the kitchen.

Later I went back to check on things. Officer Piper was still sitting on the floor beside our toilet, his hound dog eyes droopier than ever. Now his right hand held the rat in the toilet. His left one rested in his lap, all red and wrinkled.

"He'll come up any minute now." He didn't act like he believed it himself.

There was a very loud knock at the door. Before I got there, it got even louder. I opened the door.

A couple of huge TV cameras, with two men behind them, stared at me. Four guys were lugging boxes and coils of black cable and rolling tripods to our door. They had to push through a jam of staring neighbors.

Zoom Zoubek shuffled in and announced importantly, "Now here are a few reporters and television people to find out about the snake, eh. Could you let them in, eh?"

I had just opened my mouth to answer when they all pushed past me into our apartment.

The circus had begun.

Chapter

6

"HERE IS TONIGHT'S LOCAL NEWS. RESIDENTS OF the William Osler Apartments don't like their creepy new tenant. He's eight feet long, and he keeps popping up in bathrooms.

" 'He' is a boa constrictor. The slithery serpent was first discovered yesterday by ten-year-old Oliver Sullivan. . . ."

It was only the afternoon, but they were already taping tonight's news broadcast in my living room.

The tanned lady talking into the microphone looked so beautiful and sounded so smart. Who would believe that she had ground out her cigarette in our bathroom sink just before the cameras turned toward her?

I looked around our bathroom and the hall. There were a couple of paper cups on the rug and McDonald's hamburger wrappers in the bathtub.

"S.P.C.A. Officer Pat Piper says the deadly reptile is able to survive because of an air-lock in the system. He explained that it could live there for several weeks, depending on when it ate its last meal. In case it does get hungry, Piper is dangling a rat . . ."

The camera zoomed in on Officer Piper. He smiled. Just ten minutes ago he had been shouting at the TV crews and reporters to stay quiet, to turn the lights down, to stop pushing.

They laughed at him.

"What are you going to do with it when it comes up? Make leather belts?" someone teased him.

The TV announcer was finishing. "Residents are stepping carefully and looking before they sit, but they remain cheerful. 'It's just one of those things,' says—"

D.K.'s grandmother has bought every can of Drain Blaster around. We have a new tenants' committee—Bag The Boa. Its members have plastered signs all over the building. They are picketing the superintendent's apartment. Erwin Erwinson has phoned the mayor and the entire city council.

The camera crews from another station began to set up.

"Hey, Pat. Hold the rat up higher. I need a close-up shot."

"Move your head out of the way."

"Someone get rid of those shower curtains. They're in the way."

My mom sewed those.

One camera operator, with bushy red hair and a bristly red mustache, saw the expression on my face.

"Leave the curtains alone," he called to them.

He grinned at me. "These guys aren't usually this bad. The deadline for the Golden Lens Award is coming up, so they're all a bit crazy to win."

He let me hold his camera while he climbed up on our counter to film our toilet.

"Where'd this snake come from, anyway?" A fat lady from *The Country Questioner* was asking her one-millionth question.

Pat Piper stared at her. His brown hound dog eyes now seemed like those of a dog who's used to being kicked. "We're checking that out, ma'am. It takes a while. No one's rushing up to claim it."

"Why not? Exotic snakes must cost a lot."

"Because it's illegal to keep these snakes in Bay City. It'll cost someone a trip to court and a fine of up to two thousand dollars."

A reporter wearing a shiny purple baseball cap with buttons stuck all over it called out, "What kind of a weirdo owns a boa, anyway?"

Pat Piper straightened up tall. "I do," he answered with dignity.

It took all of the reporters five minutes to quiet down.

"I've had Rosie for three years," explained Officer Piper. "Found her in a warehouse when she was a baby. She had stowed away in a bunch of bananas from South America."

"I thought only tough guys kept deadly snakes," said the fat lady.

"You only hear about the bad snake owners. Just like you only know about bad pit bull terriers."

"They make better news," said the red-haired camera operator, who winked at me.

"Most exotic snake owners are responsible. It's hard work caring for them. They need to stay warm, around eighty-five, but out of the hot sun. They need vitamins, UV lights, mite protector, a 'hot rock,' thermometers, the right food—"

"Like that frozen rat?"

"And live mice, and—"

"So how do they escape?"

"Carelessness. Some cages don't close properly. Usually the owner falls asleep while playing with the snake outside the cage. Then off goes the boa. They head straight for the wallboards—"

"Keep talking. This makes great background info." The purple-capped reporter was writing fast.

"Back in behind the wallboards, they can crawl the length and width of the building. When they're hungry, they just pop into anyone's apartment."

"Coffee's here," called a cheery voice from my front door.

Everyone rushed out. Some were leaving, and others were heading for the living room. The fat lady reporter took her coffee and two chocolate doughnuts back to the bathroom.

"Pat. A doughnut? How do you take your coffee? Ollie, come have a jelly doughnut."

I liked the red-haired man.

And I liked all of this action.

I was watching the news being made. I was the news! Sort of.

Their energy was awesome. They only stood still long enough to take pictures. Otherwise they were running in and out, scribbling notes, fighting for the phone, shouting into the receiver, insulting each other, recording, filming, taping.

The excitement burst from them till it

filled our apartment and bounced back from the walls into me. It was thrilling.

Sometimes I had to make sure they would notice me. I had my *Guinness Book of World Records* handy. I'd holler out something like, "The longest poisonous snake is the King Cobra. It will attack anyone, even other cobras," and, "The Gaboon viper's fangs are so long that one at the Philadelphia Zoo actually bit himself to death." That got them nervous.

Then they would all swarm over to me, fire questions, and pop flashbulbs in my face. Ah, fame.

I couldn't believe how many pictures they took. They had two or three cameras clicking all the time.

"All those photos," I told Kathleen later. "And only one little one in the newspapers. What a waste."

They hopped on the counter, stood in the sink, lay on the floor, anything to get just the right angle. I waited for them to swing from the shower rod.

Neat words like *zoom in, pan left, that's a take,* and *cut* flew around the room.

I was trying to remember everything, to tell the guys at school.

"What are you doing home, anyway? Shouldn't you be in school?" The red-haired cameraman sat down beside me.

"I creamed the gym teacher."

I wanted to shock him, not tell him my troubles.

"Did he deserve it?"

He was so easy to talk to. He knew just the right questions to ask. Before I knew it, I had blabbed out half my life story to the red-haired cameraman, and I didn't even know his name.

He seemed to understand. He said he was divorced, too, and his boys lived with their mom.

"I'm lucky. I see them twice a wee—"

"Eeeeek! Eiiiaay!"

The glass-breaking screech from the bathroom sent my doughnut flying.

"It's here! I got it!" The fat lady reporter was squealing at the top of her lungs.

Everyone jumped to grab the cameras.

"Shoot! I missed him. You scared him away," we could hear Pat Piper shouting at her.

We raced down the hall to the bathroom.

"But I got its picture. I got it. I got it," she sang.

A mess of arms and legs and bodies got stuck in the bathroom doorway again.

Pat Piper was on his knees in front of the toilet. He acted like he was about to jump on and chew up the fat lady reporter.

She was still singing, "I got the picture, and you guys didn't!"

Finally the arms and legs and bodies pushed into the bathroom. The fat lady hugged her camera and slipped out the door.

"I'm off to develop this. Watch for it in my newspaper, *The Country Questioner*."

"I hate that woman," growled ten guys in the bathroom, in ten different ways.

Pat Piper's face was bright red. His eyes bulged. He looked more like a bulldog than a hound now. "That woman. I almost had the boa until she screeched."

51

He glared at the other newspeople. "At least we know for sure he's there. It's time for tougher tactics."

Pencils flew out. Everyone fiddled with dials and things on the cameras.

"Lay it on us, Pat."

"We'll plug an electric blanket in here, near the toilet. We put another rat on it."

I was glad we didn't own any electric blankets.

"So what's to stop the snake from grabbing the food and taking off again?"

"Simply this. I take off the toilet . . ."

"Beats cleaning it."

Pat Piper snarled at the interruption. "There'll be a hole in the floor the size of a grapefruit. I'll tape a special valve onto the hole. The snake will get his head through it, but not back out again. He'll be stuck there till I catch him."

"Sounds smooth."

"And the best part of it is"—he smiled with his teeth at the waiting pack of newspeople—"the snake will only come into a quiet room. So every one of you will have to clear up, get out, and stay out."

Someone tossed an empty paper cup at him. Everyone grumbled, but he stood, grinning, like the mutt who ate the meatballs.

The reporters and photographers all left, complaining and promising to come back anyway.

Then I noticed that a couple of the people in our apartment hadn't been newspeople at all. They were nosy neighbors.

Old Weeble from down the hall was fast asleep and snoring in our big soft TV chair. A half-eaten doughnut was still in his hand.

"How long has he been here?" I asked Officer Piper, who was putting on a brown sweater with dog hairs all over it.

"I've been in the bathroom all day." He shrugged.

I checked the clock. Kathleen and my mom were due home soon. I couldn't move old Weeble, so I cleaned up around him.

Another knock at the door. It was Gawa Luciano Cheng.

"Hi." His shiny braces flashed at me.

53

"Were you bored staying home alone all day?"

"Are you kidding? Everybody but a couple of movie stars came in here today. The boa popped out again."

"Lucky you. Tell me what happened."

I told it good.

Then I asked, "What's everybody saying about me at school?"

Just then, my mom came home.

"This mess! Oliver, what have you done?"

She was winding up for a long and loud one, when Gawa spoke to her. "Mrs. McPinkle sent me with some work for Ollie. She said to tell him she hopes everything will be straightened out soon."

"Oh, thank you. Who are you?"

"Gawa Cheng, Mrs. Sullivan. I live on the fifth floor." He stuck out his hand to shake my mom's.

"Pleased to meet you, Gawa. Why haven't we met before?"

I saw her brain in action. She was wondering how she'd missed such a polite kid, and hoping it would rub off on me.

"Come in, Gawa. Stay and show Ollie his schoolwork. Would you like some cookies?"

On her way to the kitchen, my mom noticed old Weeble still snoring in the easy chair.

"What's he doing here? Ollie, what is going on around here?"

Her timing was perfect. I pointed to the TV. The news had begun, and our bathroom was the main event.

Kathleen came in. All of us stood in a circle, watching our toilet on TV.

"Incredible," my mom said at least three times.

She wrinkled her nose, as if something smelled. "Ugh, that awful wallpaper. If I'd known everyone in Bay City was going to see it, I'd have bought that pretty new paper on sale down at Bailey's."

"You could still buy me a new sweater, in case they film me tomorrow." Kathleen is quick.

"Nice try, Sis." I broke off a piece of old Weeble's doughnut and tossed it at her.

My mom was still staring at the television.

"The yellow towels. Those ratty old yellow towels! Ollie, you could have put out some better towels."

"Mom, there's a boa in the bathroom. Who's going to notice our towels?"

"You'd be surprised."

"Don't worry, Mom. You'll have another chance to show off your good towels. They promised to be back tomorrow. It should be even wilder."

Chapter

7

"IN BAY CITY THE BIG BOA HUNT CONTINUES."

We were in the news again.

"The plan to capture the renegade reptile has backfired. While newspeople agreed to stay out of the bathroom, the sneaky serpent struck. He slithered through the special valve that should have trapped him, stole the bait, and escaped again."

Boy, did the newspeople hoot and cheer when they heard that.

"Great trap, Pat. Are you going to patent it?"

"It should earn you millions."

It was Saturday. More reporters and photographers had come, from farther away. I was answering the phone to French, Spanish, and Japanese voices yelling questions at me.

Last night my mom looked in the fridge for the fried chicken she'd had ready for supper. It was gone. We never did find out who ate it. Was it reporters, old Weeble, or some other tourist wandering around?

Kathleen and I sat squished in a corner of the living room, watching the action.

"We could make money selling them lemonade, Kathleen."

"Sure. They'd spill it all over the rug. Look at the mess now. There's a cigarette burn, too." She pointed at the carpet, then across the room. "Looks like the park after a rock concert. Hey, Ollie, watch Mom. She's talking to that red-haired cameraman again."

"Ah, he talks to everybody."

"Who is he?"

"John Lindstrom. With Channel Eight, here in Bay City. He's okay."

"Mom laughs too much when she's with him. He does, too."

"So why not? She's pretty good-looking."

I watched my mom for a while. She has soft, wavy brown hair and gentle eyes, just like Kathleen. It's me who got stuck with hair that grows straight down, and a lazy left eye.

Kathleen had gotten her purse and was leaving.

"I'm off to the mall with Rosa. See you later, you great little dodgeball player, you."

My mom rushed over to give Kathleen more advice. "Promise me you won't go near those washrooms at the mall, Kathleen."

"Maawhm."

"You never know who's down there. Those washrooms are dangerous."

"Yeah, and ours isn't."

"Kathleen."

I decided to try my luck again.

"Can't I go out, too? Just for a while, Mom?"

"If you're suspended from school, you can't go running around the streets."

"But it's Saturday."

"We talk to your principal on Monday. Then you can go out again—maybe."

"But I need fresh air."

"Open the windows."

"It's too crowded in here."

"Your room's empty. Go do your homework in it."

"I have to have some exercise first."

"Then go downstairs and get the laundry out of the dryer."

"Have I told you how sparkly and pretty you look today?"

"Downstairs, kiddo."

I came out of the laundry room lugging a heavy basket of clothes. Near the elevator, I nearly bumped into D.K. He smelled like a dirty ashtray.

"Still got the big bad snake in the can, Bawlie?"

I had managed a boa constrictor and dozens of newspeople in my apartment. I could handle D.K. "Still smoking in the storage room, D.K.?"

"Do I owe you a punch for anything?"

"Should I tell your grandma about your secret smoking room?"

"The guys at school bet you're scared stupid and crying about the snake."

I ignored him and quickly pushed the elevator button.

"Rambeau's out to get you Monday. He's going to make you fail grade five. Keep you back with the little grade fours."

The elevator doors finally opened. I rushed in. I tripped and fell into the elevator. As the door closed, D.K. was laughing wildly and I was sitting on the floor with blouses and underwear hanging all over me. I was worried sick about failing grade five.

When the elevator door opened at the front lobby, I could hear the shouting from our apartment.

Mrs. Alexopoulos was waiting by the front doors of the building with a brown suitcase beside her.

"I'm staying at my daughter's until this is over. I can't stand it anymore."

I tried to look sympathetic.

"I'm afraid to use my bathroom. I've run out of bleach to pour in my toilet. The halls are filled with rude, loud people. Why did you ever call those TV stations in the first place, Ollie?"

"Me?"

"Why aren't they catching that horrible snake, Ollie?"

The door to my apartment opened wider. Now we could really hear them fighting.

"They have a new plan, Mrs. Alexopoulos," I said.

"Another winner?"

"The owner of Noah's Pet Shop made this plan."

She glared at me as if everything were my fault, and then turned to look out the glass doors.

I escaped into our apartment. There, the yelling was impossible. Pat Piper and his boss from the S.P.C.A. were there, and they were really mad. So were the newspeople.

Pat's boss was as big and brown as a bear. "Yes, we're throwing you out," he growled. "We can't rescue this boa with you fools stomping and shouting and flashing around in here. Only Channel Eight and *The Bay City Star* stay. All you others, get out."

"And if we don't go?" asked the purple-capped reporter.

"Then we leave—and tell the public how you've prevented us from doing our jobs here. Now"—he rolled up his sleeves exposing his thick, hairy arms—"who wants to argue with me?"

I carried the clothes basket to my mom's room. She sat on the floor, putting on her shoes, crying.

"I'm not staying here. I can't watch this. I don't want to listen to it scream."

"What scream?"

"The guinea pig. They've got a little guinea pig. It's fluffy and it's shaking."

"Where? Why?"

"In a cage. On the bathroom floor. I can't stay here."

She ran out to the hall. John Lindstrom saw her, and he followed her.

I peeked into the bathroom at the brown and white guinea pig in the cage. "What are you going to do with him?" I asked Officer Piper.

"He's the new bait. We leave him here,

alone. The bars in the cage are too close for him to get out, but big enough for the boa to get in."

"Oh, no. Ugh."

"The snake crawls in. Eats the guinea pig. Becomes too fat to squeeze out again. Bingo. We got him."

I felt sick.

In the living room most of the newspeople were packing up to leave. They were still yelling and arguing with the S.P.C.A. officers. It was worse than the playground at recess. Someone bumped into a table. The vase I had given my mom for Christmas fell over and cracked into pieces.

I cut up an apple and took it to the guinea pig in the bathroom. Then I went across the hall to the Krokowskis' apartment and into their bathroom.

It was still steamy and warm. Mr. Krokowski had just left for work on the afternoon shift. I closed the toilet seat lid, sat down, closed my eyes, and held my head in my hands.

A long time later I felt calmer. I looked

around the bathroom. Mr. Krokowski's big blue bath towel hung over the shower rod, drying. His razor lay by the sink. The room smelled like a man—shaving cream, deodorant, aftershave lotion.

How I missed those things in our bathroom. Even the little black specks of hair in the sink made me sad. I leaned back on the tank and sat very still. I let the warmth and peace and smells of someone else's dad comfort me.

Outside the bathroom door, I heard Mrs. Krokowski clear her throat a lot. It was time to leave and go back to my noisy apartment.

"Hey, Ollie."

Gawa called me from the other end of the hall.

"My dad brought a great new video game home from his store. Want to play it?"

"Sure."

I was glad not to have to go back home just yet. Besides, Gawa was fun. Up to now, the only kids who seemed to like me were the kind who tried to sneak a peek into the girls' washroom and then giggle like dorks.

We took the stairs up to Gawa's floor.

"Last week I saw Borko checking out all the fire hoses hanging up in here," he said.

"That's weird even for him."

"I haven't seen him around lately. Have you?"

"That's funny. His van hasn't been out in its usual spot. What's the new game?"

"Jungle Master. Looks awesome."

We slipped the Jungle Master cartridge into the system.

"Let's start with the easy level till we get the hang of it. Then, zippo, level three."

A little man in a green camouflage suit and a safari hat marched through the jungle. Right away tigers jumped at him. Alligators attacked from behind. Jungle Master chopped up all of them.

"Piece of cake." I smiled.

A snake flashed down from the branches and struck him. Zap. Jungle Master lay flat on the ground. A little white angel floated down and sat on his chest.

"I can't escape the snakes, the slimy creeps!" I shouted.

"They're not slimy."

"What?"

"They're not slimy. They're not even wet."

"How do you know?"

"I touched one."

"When?"

"At the zoo in London, where we used to live. I went there a lot just after my baby sister was born. A couple of the zookeepers became my friends."

"You touched a snake?" I shivered. "What was it like?"

"I was surprised the first time. It was dry— and cool."

"And dirty?"

"Clean as glass."

"But scaly?"

"Only if you slide your hand up the wrong way. The other way, it's kind of soft. Like touching my mom's leather purse. Just after

67

they shed their old skin, they feel like velvet."

I looked at Gawa with great respect. "Weren't you scared it would bite?"

"Yeah. A bit. The zookeepers said there's more chance of getting bitten by a dog. Snakes are terrified of us, too."

"I know they bite people."

"Sure, if they think you're food, or if they're cornered—just like any animal would. They'd rather you went away."

"Is that why rattlesnakes rattle their tails when someone comes near?"

"I guess so."

I jumped up in surprise. A man had suddenly started singing so loud, it shook the room.

"What's that?"

"My mom's records. She loves opera singing. That's where I got my dumb middle name—Luciano."

We turned back to Jungle Master, level three.

Beasts and snakes, spears and spiders popped out all over the screen. The little man in the camouflage suit did his best, but every once in a while he'd end up on the ground, with the little angel sitting on his chest.

A giant snake with humongous dripping fangs had just done him in. I was losing.

"At least boa constrictors don't kill you with poison fangs. They coil around you and crush you to a pulp."

"Wrong again. They don't crush anything. They squeeze tighter and tighter, until there's no room for you to breathe anymore. You suffocate."

My neck started to feel tight. I coughed a lot.

"That's why they didn't let me near the big pythons and anacondas at the zoo. They would've wrapped me up in no time."

Just then Gawa's mother came into the room. She was dainty and pretty. She hummed softly along with the record from the other room, and waved a big chopping knife in the air as if she were directing the music herself.

"You must be finding it hard to get dinner

with that circus down at your place. Would you like to have dinner here with us tonight?"

"Who, me? All of us?"

"All of you. Go check with your mom."

Back at our apartment, my mom had come home with John Lindstrom. She wasn't too thrilled about my being out when she got back. Kathleen, who had returned from the mall, wasn't thrilled about eating at Gawa's.

"I don't want to eat there. What do real Chinese people eat, anyway? I know it's not the stuff we get delivered," she whined.

"I don't know, either. But it's got to be better than staying here."

"It'll be fine, Kathleen. It's nice of them to invite us," my mom said.

"What if I can't eat it? What if it's disgusting? What if we have to use chopsticks?"

"Why are you so worried? You know lots of kids from other countries."

"But I've never eaten at their houses. And besides, none of them just got here off the boat three months ago."

"Kathleen!" My mom was disgusted. "I

thought I'd raised you better than that. Have you forgotten that your own grandmother, Oma Wessberge, came here on a boat, too?"

Kathleen was embarrassed. "All right. I'm sorry. I can't think straight anymore. We haven't been alone, forever. Every time I look, someone's flashing a camera in my face. Our fridge is empty. I can't even use my own bathroom. . . ."

"Cheer up, Kathleen." I grinned. "It could have been worse."

"How?"

"You could have the forty-eight-hour flu."

She threw a pillow at me.

"Go tell Mrs. Cheng we'll be glad to come up for dinner," said my mom. "Find out when."

When I came back downstairs, Zoom, the superintendent, was just going into our apartment. He looked very serious. He headed straight toward the people bunched nervously around our bathroom door.

Pat Piper had his hand on the doorknob. He and his boss were going to check the bathroom. For once, our apartment was as silent as a grave. We all waited, afraid to blink. It was almost four o'clock now. The guinea pig had been in there for a few hours—waiting.

What would we find behind that door?

Chapter

8

PAT PIPER OPENED THE DOOR SLOWLY. I HELD MY hands to my eyes, then moved them to my stomach. I couldn't swallow. I think my heart had stopped beating.

The door creaked open. In the cage sat the guinea pig, calmly munching on my apple. The boa? We couldn't see him anywhere.

The photographer took a picture of the live guinea pig. My mom, Kathleen, and I looked at one another—and smiled.

"He's safe," my mom whispered.

Then we realized what that meant. The snake was still on the loose. The reporter and photographer and TV people would stay. No bathroom again for another night.

"I never thought I'd miss that ugly little room so much," muttered Kathleen.

"I think he's gone," announced Pat Piper's boss. "He'd be out here otherwise."

"We'll soon find out, eh. I'll be right back." Zoom left quickly and returned a minute later. I've never seen him move so fast. He was carrying a long-handled thing. A sort of a steel rope was hanging from it—a plumber's snake. I saw one before, when my little cousin plugged up our toilet with a Lego block.

"Now this'll tell us if and where that snake is, eh. I should have used it sooner."

"Oh, no, you don't!" yelled Pat Piper.

"Oh, yes, I do," Zoom yelled back.

Officer Piper and his boss stood between Zoom and the toilet. Piper grabbed the end of the plumber's snake, and held it up for us to see.

"See this hook?"

Zoom grinned. "Smart, eh? That'll grab

that snake all right. Then one good tug, eh, and, whamo. I pull him out."

"The hook will cut right into him. It'll kill him." Pat Piper and his boss looked upset.

"So what? It's only a snake, eh."

"It's a living animal."

"It shouldn't be in our toilets, eh."

"It's doing what is natural for a snake. Why should it be punished for having a sloppy owner?"

"Oh, all right." Zoom twisted the hook off.

Pat Piper's boss was still doubtful, but he let Zoom go ahead. Zoom pushed the plumber's snake into the toilet to find the real snake. We watched the snake inching down into the hole. We waited.

Zoom had reached the end of his snake— fifteen feet.

Nothing.

The boa was no longer in our toilet or in our pipes.

I jumped up and cheered. Then I saw the faces around me. Mrs. Eduardo, Erwin Erwinson, the Capellis, all looked white. If the snake wasn't there anymore, where was it?

"It could be in my bathroom." Mrs. Capelli moaned out loud what they were all thinking.

As if they were in a race, they ran out to warn the rest of the building.

Then the phone started ringing. We just couldn't answer it anymore.

"Let's get out of here," groaned my mom. She turned to Pat Piper and his boss.

"You're in charge. Try to keep some of the extras out of here. We're up in five-oh-five if you need us."

She opened our door.

Two people were already there, hands up, ready to knock. Others stood in the hall. They all talked at once.

"It's gone from your place."

"Where is it now?"

"I thought they were going to catch it this time?"

"This is outrageous."

"Our lives are in danger."

We kept quiet and walked straight toward the elevator. By the tight way my mom held her mouth, I knew she was really upset.

Kathleen looked ready to cry. If she did, I might, too.

We scurried into the elevator and shut the doors on everyone. Ah, a few seconds of beautiful quiet.

When we got to 505, Mrs. Cheng took one look at us and led us to the living room without talking. Quickly she brought us each a cup of sweet mint tea.

I felt better. Kathleen looked at Laura-Lee's shining long, black hair, and smiled at her. My mom relaxed back into the cushions of her chair. Gawa and I went to his room.

"Let's play anything but Jungle Master," I begged.

We played Karate Kid, but it was no good. We couldn't concentrate. Somehow we ended up talking about what was really on our minds—snakes.

Gawa knew everything about them. He reads a lot, and he must have almost lived at that zoo in London.

"Oh, yeah," he was answering me, "an adult boa can swallow birds, squirrels, ducks, rabbits, little dogs, or even a small wild pig, whole. That's because its jaws aren't like ours."

I opened my mouth as wide as I could.

"Its jaws are like elastic hinges. It can stretch them apart till its mouth opens really huge. Once the animal is in its mouth, its muscles start squeezing it back toward its stomach."

Finally I asked him something I've always wondered about.

"Hey, Gawa, how do snakes fool around?"

"Fool around?"

"You know . . ."

"Oh. The male boa—"

"Science is interesting, isn't it, boys." Mrs. Cheng had come to call us for dinner. My face turned tomato red.

"In honor of our guests, we're having American food today. Hot dogs." She smiled.

I was still feeling red when we got to the table.

Kathleen was sitting beside Laura-Lee. Laura-Lee's hair was all braided. Kathleen loves playing hairdresser. She adores anyone with long hair. Beside her was Gawa's baby sister in a high chair. His dad and grandfather sat across from them.

Kathleen pointed at the knives and forks on the table and grinned happily at me. Only Gawa's grandfather had chopsticks. I thought it would have been fun to try them.

"Here we are."

My mom and Mrs. Cheng carried the plates in.

On our plates were big piles of steaming rice, vegetables, and the hot dogs. They were cut up in little pieces. Mrs. Cheng looked so proud, I knew I shouldn't ask for a hot dog bun—or ketchup.

I watched Gawa's grandfather eat. He was using his chopsticks better than I use my fork. He didn't have a plate. He ate from a fancy bowl with designs painted all around it. I guess he didn't speak English, but he smiled at me every time he noticed me staring at him.

"Why does your grandfather use a bowl?" I whispered to Gawa.

"You always get a bowl when you use

79

chopsticks. You'd make a real mess eating from a plate."

He looked at me like I was a space case. For the first time, it occurred to me that sometimes people might think some of the things we think and do are strange.

That meal was the happiest time we'd had in days. I've never heard a dad tell so many jokes. Even my mom told one. Luckily, Kathleen didn't.

It was time to go much sooner than I wanted.

"That felt like a week's vacation," my mom said as we walked down the hall.

"I hate to find out what's happened at our place while we were gone." Kathleen can be so cheerful.

D.K.'s grandmother came down the hall toward us, looking really worried.

"Have you seen D.K.?"

"No."

"I can't find him anywhere."

That should be good news, I thought to myself.

Then I noticed her face. It was blotchy red.

Her nose started to wiggle up and down. I knew she was trying not to cry.

"I've phoned everyone he knows. I've searched everywhere. He's gone. Maybe that horrible snake ate him. My little guy."

Then she did cry.

It's tough trying to imagine D.K. as someone's "little guy."

"If we see him, we'll call you right away," my mom promised.

Something started to bother me, but I kept quiet.

Our apartment was almost empty. Only the red-haired cameraman, John Lindstrom, and Officer Piper were talking seriously with two men and a lady.

They turned out to be the owner of our building, a city councilman, and the mayor. They were planning the next action to take.

My mom bustled around making coffee. Kathleen disappeared to the Krokowskis' bathroom. I plopped into a chair. I listened to the discussion and let my conscience bother me.

I knew where D.K. probably was.

But why should I find him? He'd done nothing for me but ruin my life.

I couldn't get the picture of his grandmother looking sick with worry out of my head.

I slipped out of our apartment to find her and tell her where D.K. might be. I thought again. He'd kill me if I told about his secret smoking room. I decided to go down to get him myself.

The halls in the basement are still and creepy at night. I didn't like the long thin shadows.

There was the gray door to the storage room. It was wedged slightly open with an empty cigarette package. The room was quiet.

I pushed the door open wider. The cigarette package fell down to the floor. At first the dim room seemed empty. Then I saw him.

D.K. was flattened against the far wall of the room. His eyes, wide open, stared straight ahead. He stood like he was frozen solid. Why was he acting so weird?

I stepped into the room. Then I saw why D.K. was so scared.

Coiled up beside the drain hole in the middle of the floor was the boa. It looked big and brown and slimy. And it lay between D.K. and the door where I stood.

The door! It was closing. Fast.

I jumped back to it just as it slammed shut. I jiggled the rusty old handle.

This could not be true. It was stuck shut.

We were locked in. Just D.K. and me—and a six-foot boa constrictor.

Chapter

9

"SSSTUPID SLOB."

At first I thought the hiss from across the room was from the snake.

"What did you do that for?"

Then I realized it was D.K. trying to whisper.

"I'm madder than you are. I only came down here 'cause your grandma's worried."

"You told my grandmother my secret get-away! I'll pun—"

"I should have told her." I didn't bother to point out to him that he couldn't get across the room to punch me. There was a snake between us.

"Tattletale! Blabbermouth. Bawlie Ollie."

"I should have told, because then someone would know where we are. Then they could come down here to get us out."

"Why didn't you tell her, you manure-brain?"

"Bag your tongue for a minute. You're too scared to know what you're saying. I would be, too, if a deadly boa constrictor were creeping up on me—" I stopped talking—horrified. I realized that the snake really was getting closer. D.K. saw it too.

He flattened himself against the wall until he looked as if someone had drawn him on the cement with white chalk. Only his mouth moved. It opened wide, but no sound came out.

Watching the snake crawl was as fascinating as watching a horror movie. The movement started in the tail, then oozed forward in curves, till suddenly, the head was a few inches ahead. Closer to D.K.

I don't like D.K. But I didn't want to watch him getting choked and eaten by a snake.

Should I throw something at it? I looked

around the room. There were boxes and old paint cans. Nothing here could kill the boa right away. Anything else would just make him come after me. Even me moving around too fast could cause that.

Gawa had explained that to me. Moving fast is the worst thing to do around a snake. Snakes don't see or hear too well. They find things by sensing temperatures. Animals and people give off heat. Moving animals and people give off even more heat.

The snake stopped. It lifted its wide head. I knew its tongue would be flicking out and in. Checking out its prey.

What do guys in movies do in these situations? I thought hard.

D.K. was stretched flat beside a bunch of pipes leading up the wall to the apartments above. I shivered. It was cold down here.

Cold! That was it! The snake wasn't aiming for D.K. It was searching for warmth. The hot water pipes next to D.K., not D.K.

"Hey jelly-guts," I whispered across the room. "He doesn't want you. Even snakes have taste. Move away. Move really slowly—so you won't attract him."

D.K. couldn't hear me. He was just like a wax dummy in a museum.

"D.K., move! Now. Before it crawls any closer."

I knew he wouldn't. He was too scared. I'd have to go over to help him.

Me? I'm a chicken. The kids at school know it—and I know it.

The snake's tail started to move forward again. In seconds its head was closer to D.K., its tongue testing the air.

D.K. began making weird noises like a kitten crying. I was afraid he'd do something dumb, like run. I had to act.

"Stay still, D.K." I was surprised how tough my voice sounded. "Don't move. I'm coming over."

Slowly, carefully, I inched my way around the room. My heart knocked so loudly, it made echoes in my head. I tried to ignore the snake and watch D.K., who was looking at me like he was drowning. I kept moving.

I reached him. The snake slithered forward

again. One more move and it would be half his length away—striking distance.

Now he had a choice of two meals.

As carefully as a cat, I reached out to D.K. Talking calmly, I took his arm. I pulled him, slowly, along the wall.

It seemed like hours before we made it to the other side of the room.

"Yikes! Ollie, look."

D.K. pointed to where we had been standing a while ago. The boa was there now. Its dark tongue flickered again.

It didn't stay there long. Up the wall it glided, right to the hot water pipes. It curled itself around them.

We were safe for now. We sat down, our backs against the cement wall. We needed to catch our breath and to think.

I could not relax. Not when I knew I was a prisoner in a little room with a giant snake that was now stretched out along the hot water pipes like a sunbather at the beach.

When would he come down for a snack?

"Now what do we do? I want to get out of here," D.K. whined.

There's a Snake in the Toilet

"Me too. Got any ideas?"

"Let's try the door again."

"May as well."

This felt funny. I had been sitting beside D.K. for quite a while. We were talking and planning together. He hadn't sworn at me, or punched me, or even threatened to punch me. Amazing.

"Remember, move slowly," I said.

We tried the door handle. We jiggled and pushed, and lifted and pulled. It would not budge.

"We're making too much noise. We'll attract the snake, Ollie."

"Someone outside might hear us. Couldn't we yell for help through the keyhole?"

"Nobody ever comes down to this part of the basement. No one over in the laundry room could hear us because of the noise of the machines. Besides, it's too risky." He pointed at the sunbathing boa.

We panicked.

"What do we do? What do we do?" said D.K.

89

"It might be days or weeks before anyone comes down here."

"They'll find us dead."

"If they find anything at all."

"Why won't anyone come to help us?"

"Oh, why didn't I tell my mom I was coming down here?"

That was when I came closest to crying. I had to keep talking. "Let's think. Moving around too much is dangerous. The door's useless."

"There's no window. No holes are big enough for us to crawl out."

"Ha. Remember that old joke Leroy told everybody? About the guy in a locked room with a baseball and bat?"

"Yeah. He hit three strikes and he was out."

"I forgot my ball, too."

We sat in gloomy silence, feeling sorry for ourselves. What a way to go. We were either going to starve—or be eaten.

I checked out the room again. I was wearing out my brain, thinking so hard.

"That's it!" I yelled out loud.

"Are you going delirious on me already? Calm down, dummy."

"D.K., I've got it. The fusebox," I whispered this time, and pointed to the fusebox on the wall to the left of the door.

"What are you going to do, electrocute the snake?"

I moved slowly toward the fuse box. D.K. followed. It was still the old-fashioned kind, like everything else in our building. The box was about two feet tall and a foot wide. Two rows of fuses, the little, round glass kind, were inside. Some were labeled Air Conditioners, Bk. Stairs. Most were too faded to read or had weird short forms—Pf Rm. Some had nothing at all. Good old organized Zoom.

"This is what will bring someone down here."

"Why would anyone come down here at night to check the fuse box?"

"If the lights went off."

D.K. looked at me as if he'd been shot.

"The—the lights—off? In here, too?"

I hadn't thought of that.

I read the labels on the fuses, praying to

find the one for the first floor. This sure wasn't my lucky day.

"It's a chance we'll have to take."

"How?"

"I'll unscrew a few and hope the lights go off wherever Zoom is."

"And hope they won't go off in here?"

"Yeah."

"No way! I'm not sitting here in the dark, wondering where that snake is."

I had to agree. We slid to the floor below the fuse box. We sat. We waited. And waited. There was nothing to wait for. No one knew we were down here. No one was coming to help us.

"Oh, no!" D.K. grabbed my arm, hard, and jumped up.

"What? What?"

"It's moving again!"

I felt like a claw had squeezed my throat from the inside. The pipes must have got too hot for the boa. It had uncurled itself from them and was gliding along beside the wall.

"He's coming to get us." D.K. sounded like a kitten again.

"Cool it, D.K. We're safe if we stay still."

But how long could we stay down here like this? D.K.'s eyes were getting glassy again.

"Look, D.K. We have to do it. No one's ever going to come down here otherwise. It's the only way."

D.K. was in the wax-dummy state again. He was hypnotized by the sliding six-foot snake.

It was up to me.

Could I hack it? Could I stay here in the dark, knowing the snake was somewhere near? That it could jump me any second? Would they find me scratching and screaming and crying at the door like a loony? Would they find me at all?

D.K. the kitten mewed again.

The snake lifted its head. Its forked tongue flicked out, quivered in the air, and disappeared. I knew it had no ears, but it still seemed like it was listening.

Did D.K. sound like dinner?

"Shut up, kitten-heart, manure-brain. He thinks you're food."

Again, I was amazed at how strong I sounded. D.K. obeyed me.

"I'm going to do the fuses now. No matter what happens, don't move, don't make a sound."

I stared at the fuses. I thought it was dangerous to touch them. I could electrocute myself. But I had no choice.

The first two fuses had to be the basement. I skipped those, and started to unscrew the third.

"Please, God, let number three be the main floor. Let the light in here stay on."

Relief. The light stayed on. I couldn't take any chances, though. I had to take out some more fuses—just to make sure the lights upstairs would go off where they'd be noticed right away.

I twisted out another one. I was too nervous. The fuse slipped out of my shaking hand and clattered to the floor. A shotgun blast would have been quieter.

I froze. D.K. crumpled to the floor. The fuse rolled and rolled noisily across the floor until it clunked into the drainpipe in the middle.

The boa wasn't even interested. I stayed still and counted to fifty. Then I started working on the fuses again.

On the next fuse, my luck died. The room darkened as black as a garbage bag. I held on to the wall as if it could save me.

Something clutched my pant leg. D.K. pulled himself up, and we held on to each other and cried, together.

A miracle happened. A light above us burst on. An emergency light, hooked to a huge battery. I hadn't thought of that.

We blinked. It was only a small beam, but I had never been so grateful for a light. We grinned at each other and cheered a loud, silent hurray.

"Ollie, you're smarter than I thought."

Why should I change his mind?

My smile froze. The boa was still crawling toward us. Would help come in time?

We listened desperately. Were those footsteps in the hall?

No.

The snake curved closer. We were staring straight across at its face.

It slithered under the beam of light. Its eyes glowed green like those of an angry cat. Its whole long body reflected and sparkled in the light like brown glass, with diamonds.

It would have been beautiful if it hadn't been so horrible.

And it kept coming at us. I took D.K.'s arm and pulled him with me in the other direction.

"We'll stay just close enough to the door to listen," I whispered to him.

Two things happened at the same time. I couldn't believe my crummy luck.

We heard voices and footsteps in the hall. Help was coming. At the same moment the snake reached the door.

I knew what would happen. Whoever came through the door, noisy and unsuspecting, would be attacked by that snake.

I had to stop it. What could I do?

I made everything Gawa told me about snakes and anything I'd ever read fast-forward through my mind.

I could pick it up. Carry it away from the door before it opened. If I did it right, I'd be safe.

If I did it right.

I was afraid of how the snake would feel. If it was wet and slimy after all, I'd drop it. That would be a disaster.

I was pretty sure I was big enough to hold it, but D.K. was bigger. I looked at him, shivering and shaking. Useless.

It had to be me.

The door handle jiggled.

It had to be now.

Chapter

10

~~~~~

QUICKLY I STEPPED UP TO THE SNAKE. MY RIGHT hand shot out and grabbed its narrow neck.

It squirmed, but I held on tight. I couldn't let it turn its head to bite me.

Just as its tail flipped up, I grabbed it about three feet from the end. Now its tail could wrap around my arm, but it couldn't choke me.

Was I relieved. The snake was dry. It felt like a burlap sack—or a dog's tongue—dry. I could last for a while.

Grunting and shoving, someone was pushing the door open. I stepped well back. No sense giving him a heart attack when he came in.

The door opened wide. Suddenly a bright beam from a flashlight blinded me and panicked the boa. He jerked so hard my left arm shot up in the air with it.

D.K. screeched and screeched. The flashlight smashed to the floor and the room was dark again.

Then I heard John Lindstrom speak. No voice sounded better.

"Zoom, get those lights on fast. Stop yelling, kid. You're safe now."

Light filled the room. John looked at me. Awe and admiration covered his face.

"Ollie, you've got to be the bravest fellow in the country. I couldn't do that." He shuddered.

"So how're we going to get that snake away, eh?" asked Zoom. "Ollie can't just put it down—and he sure can't go walking through the halls with it, eh."

"Good question. Let me think," said John.

I was glad they were taking over. I was concentrating so hard on holding the snake, I couldn't think about anything else.

"Zoom, bring Piper's cage down here fast.

It's in the living room. I'll stay down here with the boys."

As soon as Zoom stepped out the door, D.K. scuttled out after him. We could hear him pounding down the hall.

John was thoughtful. Then he spoke to me.

"I wanted to get my cameras and film this. It would have been a terrific scoop for me—and for you."

I pictured myself in the news on TV tomorrow. I'd have been on the front page of *The Bay City Star*. In color. It would be tacked onto every bulletin board at school. I could mail it to my dad.

"I didn't, because I want that cage down here fast. This boa's had enough agitation. By the time I ran up and brought down my equipment, the delay could be fatal. If the snake goes really crazy, you might not be safe."

I knew what he had given up for me—the prize-winning tape—the chance of a lifetime. Saying "thanks" didn't seem enough.

"I'll make sure everyone finds out how brave you are, Ollie."

Soon, Zoom was back with Pat Piper and the cage. My mom and Kathleen rushed right behind him. My mom looked gray and old. Kathleen carried a still camera.

We worked as smoothly as if we had rehearsed it. Officer Piper set the cage down and held open the door.

John snapped still pictures. He took them from off to the side, so it wouldn't excite the snake.

I sort of threw the boa into the cage, headfirst. Then I whipped my hands back fast. Pat Piper clanged the door shut.

I was safe at last.

My mom and Kathleen rushed to me. We hugged and hugged. My mother's crying made me start too. I stopped, embarrassed.

John clapped me on the shoulder.

"After tonight you can cry anytime you want. No one will ever dare doubt your courage again."

We left the snake in the room and went upstairs to our apartment. Mom wouldn't quit hugging me. Kathleen looked really impressed and asked me a million questions.

Pat Piper shook my hand, gathered his things, and said good-bye.

Apartment news travels fast. Before I finished telling Mom and Kathleen and John everything, the knocks on the door and the telephone calls began—again.

I was just too tired to care. Mom put me to bed and John sent everybody away—except D.K. and his grandmother, who came down to thank me.

So now I'm a hero. The reporters and photographers came once more. To see *me*.

The French and Spanish and Japanese phone callers were asking questions about me—Oliver Sullivan, Snake Catcher. My picture and story made the papers all over the world.

I mailed some of the articles to my dad. He phoned to say how proud he was. But he still didn't invite me to visit him in Egypt.

I don't mind, though. John Lindstrom is taking me camping with him and his sons this July.

Last night my mom told me that John is

going to be around a lot from now on. She sure looked happy.

The boa? He's at Bay City Animal Hospital right now. Four days in the toilet pipes were pretty bad for him. We'll never find out all the things that were poured on him.

We won't know for a while if he'll live or not. Poor guy. I never thought I'd feel sorry for him.

His owner turned out to be Borko. He's due in court soon, and he won't get the snake back.

Pat Piper says he'd like to take the boa home if he gets better. He's calling him Ollie. I'm not sure how I feel about that, but I really hope Ollie makes it.

I'm back in school. D.K. and Mrs. McPinkle both came with my mom and me to face the principal and Mr. Rambeau.

I have only one big problem now.

How do I get out *to* recess?

Gawa and Ian and the other guys are waiting for me.

I have a note from Zoe in my pocket. She wants me to meet her by the maple tree.

D.K. has an extra piece of cherry pie for me. We'll never be real friends, but he swears to protect me until death. Probably not because I saved him, but because I haven't told anyone what a baby he was that night in the basement.

"Please, Mrs. McPinkle. I know this math. When can I go out for recess?" I begged.

"You missed two days of schoolwork, Ollie. Hero or not, you have to catch up."

She tried to hide her smile, but I knew.

"Besides, I thought you hated recess."

"Who, me? Whatever gave you that idea? I love recess. A hurricane couldn't make me miss it."

About the Author

GISELA TOBIEN SHERMAN was born in Germany and immigrated with her family to Canada when she was six years old. She knew in grade five that she wanted to become a writer. She started her career as a teacher and then a school librarian, and now writes full-time. Gisela has published numerous articles in her local papers, has written award-winning short stories, and is the author of the book *King of the Class*. Currently she lives with her husband, three children, a cocker spaniel, a cat, and whatever animal her children bring home—except snakes—in Burlington, Ontario.

There's a Snake in the Toilet is based on an actual news event that occurred in Gisela's neighboring city, Hamilton.

BILL WALLACE

Award-winning author Bill Wallace brings you fun-filled
stories of animals full of humor and exciting adventures.

BEAUTY
RED DOG
TRAPPED IN DEATH CAVE
A DOG CALLED KITTY
DANGER ON PANTHER PEAK
SNOT STEW
**FERRET IN THE BEDROOM, LIZARDS IN THE
FRIDGE**
DANGER IN QUICKSAND SWAMP
CHRISTMAS SPURS
TOTALLY DISGUSTING
BUFFALO GAL
NEVER SAY QUIT
BIGGEST KLUTZ IN FIFTH GRADE
BLACKWATER SWAMP
WATCHDOG AND THE COYOTES
TRUE FRIENDS
JOURNEY INTO TERROR
THE FINAL FREEDOM
THE BACKWARD BIRD DOG
UPCHUCK AND THE ROTTEN WILLY
**UPCHUCK AND THE ROTTEN WILLY:
THE GREAT ESCAPE**
THE FLYING FLEA, CALLIE, AND ME

A MINSTREL® BOOK

Published by Pocket Books

648-28